Inspired by the amazing true story

Dolphin Tale™

A Tale of True Friendship

Adapted by Emma Ryan
Based upon the screenplay written by
Karen Janszen and Noam Dromi

SCHOLASTIC INC.
New York   Toronto   London   Auckland
Sydney   Mexico City   New Delhi   Hong Kong

P9-CQY-232

ISBN 978-0-545-34841-6

12 11 10 9 8 7 6 5 4   11 12 13 14 15 16/0

Printed in the U.S.A.   40
First printing, August 2011

This is the story of a friendship between a very special dolphin named Winter, and a boy named Sawyer.

One day, Sawyer was riding his bike when he saw a dolphin lying on the beach. Winter had been swimming in the ocean, but she had swum too close to the shore. Now her tail was caught in a crab trap!

Winter was in trouble. Sawyer could see the dolphin was hurt and knew he had to help her.

Sawyer remembered that he had a pocketknife in his backpack. He used the knife to cut Winter free from the trap. Winter looked at Sawyer and made a soft whistling noise, as if to say "thank you."

Soon, rescue workers from the local Marine Hospital arrived. They took Winter to the hospital. The next day Sawyer went to the hospital to visit Winter. There he met Hazel, the daughter of Dr. Haskett, the doctor who was in charge of the Marine Hospital.

Winter was in a large pool with Phoebe, one of the trainers, when Sawyer saw her. Winter had a bandage where her tail had been. Her eyes were shut and she wasn't moving.

As soon as Sawyer spoke to Phoebe, Winter opened her eyes. She looked right at Sawyer and made the soft whistling sound again! She was happy to see her friend.

Sawyer came back to visit Winter the next day. The trainers were worried because Winter still hadn't tried to swim.

But, when she saw Sawyer, Winter wiggled her body, trying to move closer to him. Sawyer slowly reached his hand out and touched Winter's head. Winter sighed. Her friend was there.

Sawyer started visiting the hospital every day. Each day, Sawyer could see Winter growing stronger. Sawyer and Hazel made special food for her to help her get better.

At night, Sawyer would research
dolphins until he fell asleep!

Winter still couldn't swim like she used to, but she floated and moved around the pool by wiggling her body and flapping her fins. She also used her fins to play games with Sawyer and splash him with water.

Winter loved to play with toys, too. She would sometimes grab a toy in Sawyer's hand with her mouth and try to pull Sawyer into the pool with her!

One day, the trainers noticed a bump on Winter's back. So Dr. Haskett took an X-ray of Winter's spine.

The X-ray showed that Winter's spinal cord was being damaged from the way she was swimming. Dolphins are supposed to swim by moving their bodies up and down, not side to side as Winter had been doing.

Dr. Haskett explained that the spinal cord in both humans and dolphins control their heart, movements, and breathing. If Winter didn't start learning how to swim by moving her body up and down again, her spinal cord could get worse. She could even die.

Sawyer was very worried for Winter.
But he had an idea . . .

Sawyer talked to his cousin Kyle, who had hurt his leg while serving in the Army. A man named Dr. McCarthy had made Kyle a plastic brace to help him walk. Kyle said that Dr. McCarthy also made legs out of plastic. These are called prosthetics. Sawyer wondered if the doctor could make Winter a prosthetic tail.

Great news! Dr. McCarthy
agreed to come and see Winter.

Dr. McCarthy's first step was to make a mold of the stump where Winter's tail used to be.

The doctor used the mold to create Winter's new tail. Once it was ready, Winter could test out her new tail.

Sawyer and everyone at the hospital were nervous to see if Winter could use her new tail. They held her in the pool as Dr. McCarthy attached the prosthetic.

They gently tried to let Winter go, but she started squealing and thrashing around. She didn't like the new tail and smashed it against the pool until it broke.

Sawyer and the others were crushed.
But Dr. McCarthy wasn't ready to give up yet.

He decided to make a different prosthetic for Winter with a better liner.

The time came to test Winter's new and improved tail. Everyone at the hospital held their breath while the prosthetic was attached.

Winter looked back at her new tail and shook it. She slowly started to move her tail up and down and up and down . . . she was swimming! Winter was going to be okay.

Thanks to the special friendship of a brave boy, and the help of some very caring people, a dolphin received a brand-new tail and learned how to swim again.